The Lullabob

Written by John Lockyer
Illustrated by Richard Hoit

Rigby

PHASE ONE

BEN IVAN stepped away from the starship and hid behind the trunk of a blimb tree. He heard cackling parrots and space squirrels moving above him and a deep, sweet humming. He touched the phaser in his belt and peered around the tree. A short, plump, purple creature was shuffling toward him.

The creature stretched out a three-fingered hand and picked a ripe blimb. It held the blimb above its head. It squeezed the moist fruit onto its tongue and swallowed. Wrinkling its squashed nose, the creature shuffled on, searching for more blimbs, before moving on toward Ben's tree.

Ben drew his phaser, and leaped forward. He stood — phaser flashing — ready to fire. The creature was unafraid. It didn't even blink. Ben waved his phaser. "Who are you?"

The creature folded its hands on its chest. "I'm the guardian of Planet Lulla. Who are you?"

"Ben Ivan, Space Patrol Officer from the United Council of Planets. I received an emergency call from this planet. The message said that a lullabob is terrorizing the land. It is destroying space sprites. I am here to save the sprites."

The creature shuffled closer to Ben and lowered its voice. "Others have been here before, you know. All have failed."

It was Ben's turn to smile. "They must have been weak and foolish."

The creature folded its hands across its chest again. "Foolish? Yes. Weak? No."

Ben gripped his phaser tightly. "The lullabob is no match for me. Where is it?"

The creature turned and pointed toward a rocky cliff. "The lullabob's den is at the end of an unmarked trail. Once on the trail you cannot turn back."

Ben waved his phaser. "Lead the way."

The creature looked pleased with itself. It shuffled up to the cliff, stepped through the rock, and disappeared. Ben swung his phaser, scanning the wall. "Where are you? Where did you go?"

The creature's voice sounded hollow and far away. "Step through the wall and you will see me."

THE COCOON

BEN TOUCHED the bare rock and was sucked forward. The rock closed around him and everything went black. For a moment he felt he was floating on air. Then there was light and he found himself on a bed of spongy white thread. The walls and ceilings were made of the same thread. Ben bounced up and down, and pushed against it. The thread stretched out . . . then shrank back. He felt like he was inside a giant cocoon.

The creature was in front of him. "Put your hand on my shoulder and I will guide you," it said.

Ben shook his head. "I want my hands free."

The creature shrugged and turned away. It waddled across the bed of thread, jiggling like jelly. Ben followed unsteadily. He couldn't see where he was going, or where he had been. The threads bulged in front of him. It was like walking inside a rolling bubble. After what seemed like days, the threads finally ended at another wall of rock.

THE LULLABOB

THE CREATURE turned to Ben. "Are you ready to meet the lullabob?" it asked.

Ben breathed hard and nodded. The creature smiled and stepped through the wall. Ben was sucked forward into darkness. He felt himself floating. Then he saw light. He landed on a grassy triangle surrounded by plants. He looked down. His phaser was gone.

Ben moved amongst the plants, searching for the rock wall. "I must have my phaser. I must go back. I can't fight the lullabob with my bare hands."

The creature sighed. "Forget your phaser. It's gone. You really don't get it, do you? Why do you think you are here?"

Ben clenched his fists. "I've already told you," he said angrily. "The emergency message."

The creature giggled. "The message was a hoax. The message came from the lullabob."

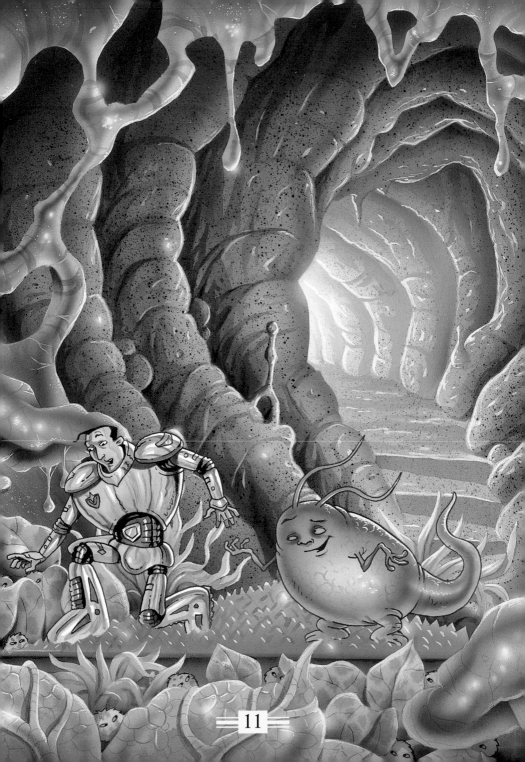

Ben was shocked. He didn't know what to say. The creature laughed. It shuffled to the mouth of a cave in the undergrowth and waved to Ben. "Come closer."

Ben took two steps forward. The creature grinned. "You see! The lullabob is unique. There is only one lullabob in this galaxy, and to survive, it must trap a human each solar cycle. So it sends an emergency message into the paths of patrolling starships. One always responds. This time it was you."

Ben Ivan didn't move. He shook his head. "No."

The creature held up a pudgy purple hand. "Don't be afraid. The lullabob sings the sweetest, purest lullabies ever heard. It sings its victims to sleep — a sleep from which they never return. Come now, come closer."

Ben stepped backward. The creature clapped its hands once. All was still. Then, slowly the plants began to quiver and rustle. Hundreds of tiny multicolored fur balls landed on the grassy triangle. They rolled and bounced and flew at Ben's face.

Ben ducked and kicked, but there were too many. They drove him toward the creature and the cave. Ben stumbled and fell to his knees. "Stop!" he shouted. "Stop!"

The creature clapped its hands twice. The fur balls rolled away back into the plants and were still.

Ben stared at them. "What are they?" he asked.

The creature grinned. "They are the lullabob's little helpers. They are the space sprites of Planet Lulla."

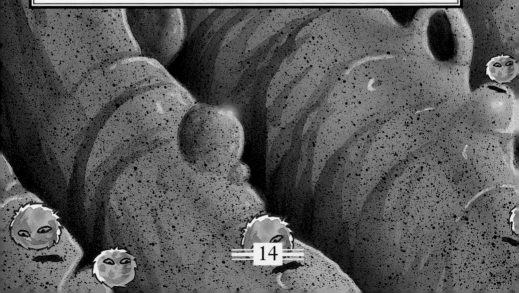

Ben looked at the creature . . . then back at the space sprites. Escape was impossible. The creature reached out and patted his arm. "Don't be scared. The lullabies of the lullabob will numb you. You won't feel a thing."

Ben shook his head, desperately trying to think of a way to escape. "You know the lullabob. Talk to it. Tell it I escaped. Why can't you help me?"

The creature gurgled. Its face softened and glowed. It hummed a little and then began a soft, sweet, silvery lullaby.

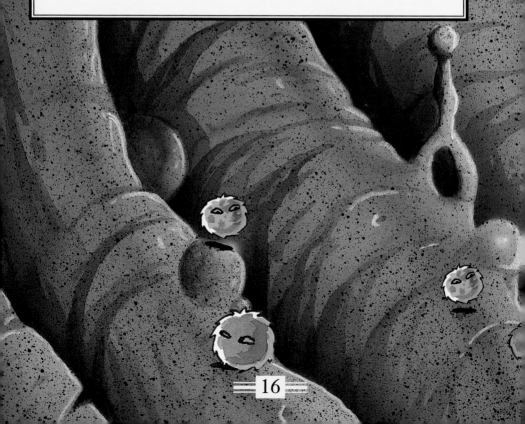

WHAT IS SCIENCE FICTION?

Science Fiction is a narrative in which the author uses scientific language and ideas to write about an imaginary futuristic world.

A science-fiction story has a plot with:
- an introduction
- a problem
- a resolution

HOW TO WRITE A SCIENCE-FICTION STORY

STEP 1

Make a *story plan* to help you organize your story.

Introduction

Who	Where	When

Who
Where
When
→
Event
Event
Event
→
Problem →

Event
Event
→
Resolution

2

Look back at your plan and write an *introduction*, using:
– *characters* from the future
– a *setting* in a futuristic imaginary world
– *scientific words:* starship, Planet Lulla, Lullabob

3

Write about the *events* of the story that led up to the *problem*.

4

Write about *what happens* as a *result* of the events, i.e., the *problem*.

5

Write about the *sequence of events* that led to the *resolution*.

6

Write about the *resolution*. Tell the reader *how* the problem was resolved.

Guide Notes

Title: The Lullabob
Stage: Fluency (4)

Text Form: Science Fiction
Approach: Guided Reading
Processes: Thinking Critically, Exploring Language, Processing Information
Written and Visual Focus: Chapter Heads

THINKING CRITICALLY
(sample questions)
- How can you tell this is a science-fiction story?
- Why do you think Ben Ivan was sent alone to face the lullabob?
- What do you think Ben could have done to save himself?
- How do you feel about the ending of the story? What do you think might have happened?

EXPLORING LANGUAGE

Terminology
Spread, author, illustrator, credits, imprint information, ISBN number

Vocabulary
Clarify: phaser, multicolored, desperately, quiver, guardian, terrorizing, sprite, scanning, hoax, solar, unique
Pronouns: he, its, you, they
Adjectives: *cackling* parrots, *short, plump, purple* creature, *squashed* nose, *spongy white* thread
Homonyms: through/threw, here/hear, know/no, where/wear
Antonyms: end/beginning, disappeared/appeared, stretch/shrink, back/forward
Synonyms: peered/looked, unique/special, stumbled/tripped
Simile: jiggling *like jelly*

Print Conventions
Apostrophe – possessive (creature's voice, Lullabob's little helpers, Lullabob's den)